The Lost Prince
A DROID™ ADVENTURE

By Ellen Weiss
Illustrated by Amador

Based on a story by Peter Sauder

RANDOM HOUSE 🏠 NEW YORK

Copyright © 1985 Lucasfilm Ltd. (LFL). All rights reserved under International and Pan-American Copyright Conventions. Published in the United States by Random House, Inc., New York, and simultaneously in Canada by Random House of Canada Limited, Toronto.

Library of Congress Cataloging in Publication Data: Weiss, Ellen. The lost prince. SUMMARY: R2-D2 and C-3PO find a new master and adventure with a lost prince in dangerous mines. 1. Children's stories, American. [1. Science fiction] I. Amador, ill. II. Title. PZ7.W4472Lo 1985 [Fic] 85-8182 ISBN: 0-394-87735-7 Manufactured in the United States of America 1 2 3 4 5 6 7 8 9 0

TM—Trademarks of LFL used by Random House, Inc., under authorization.

The frontier mining town of Tyne's Horky was a rough and rowdy place. Its streets were filled with bounty hunters, thieves, and miners who had come to search for the valuable white element called keschel. People came to Tyne's Horky to find a fortune—or to steal it from someone else. The only law was the law of the blaster.

One bright morning C-3PO and his companion R2-D2 stepped off a space freighter in Tyne's Horky. Artoo looked up and down the street, clicking and whirring nervously.

"I'll tell you what a nice pair of droids like us is doing in a place like this," replied Threepio. "You know as well as I do. The Intergalactic Droid Agency has found us employment with a new master here, and they promised it would be a clean, safe job for a maintenance droid and a translator. That is," he added, "if we can find this 'Doodnik's Café.'"

Doodnik's Café was right down the street. As soon as the two droids walked in, Doodnik put them to work. "You," he said, pointing to Threepio. "Take this drink over to that table." He handed Threepio a smoking black concoction on a tray. Then he turned to Artoo. "Go see what table three wants," he ordered. Sitting at table three was a large lizard-skinned alien with four heads. He looked mad. Artoo made a sound between a beep and a whimper and went to work.

Artoo and Threepio spent the rest of the day scurrying back and forth with orders and trying to stay out of trouble.

Later that day two men sat down at a table in Doodnik's darkest corner: a heavy man in a spotless white suit and a figure who was completely shrouded in a dark, hooded robe. Kleb Zellock, the man in white, breathed air from the tubes of an atmospheric purifier he carried over his shoulder. He wore thick goggles to protect his eyes from dust. Thanks to the purifier, his breath came in hoarse rasps, so he sounded as sinister as he looked. It was well known that Kleb hated germs and dirt. It was even better known that he was a very dangerous man.

"Tell me, Sollag," Kleb was saying to the hooded man, "juzzt what makezz thizz 'Julpa' zooo important to you?"

Sollag shook his head. "That is not your affair," he replied. "Just find him for me. I am willing to pay you a fortune if you succeed—forty thousand grains of keschel."

"Zooo be it," said Kleb. "If I can't find himmm, nooo one cann. Izzzn't that right, Yorpo?" he said, turning to a hulking figure behind him.

The figure who stood behind Kleb was Yorpo Mog, Kleb's faithful henchman. Yorpo looked about as different from Kleb as could be. He was eight feet tall and covered with several years' worth of filth. Yorpo Mog *never* took a bath.

Yorpo grunted in agreement. "You find," he snorted.

At that moment Threepio arrived with a huge platter of food for Kleb's table. He was moving fast, too fast to see Yorpo's giant toenail in his path. He tripped, lurched forward, and crashed into Yorpo Mog's knees. Yorpo went down and landed with his face in Kleb's dinner. Enraged, Yorpo sent Threepio flying across the room with a kick and then charged after him.

"Juzzt a minute, Yorpo," interrupted Kleb. "You have work to do. Go and zzzee what you cann find for meee at the auction." Reluctantly, Yorpo wiped his face and lumbered out of the café.

Threepio was left lying in a heap of broken crockery. "Don't worry," he said to Artoo, "our master knows it wasn't our fault."

Thirty seconds later they had been hurled into the street. "And don't come back!" shouted Doodnik.

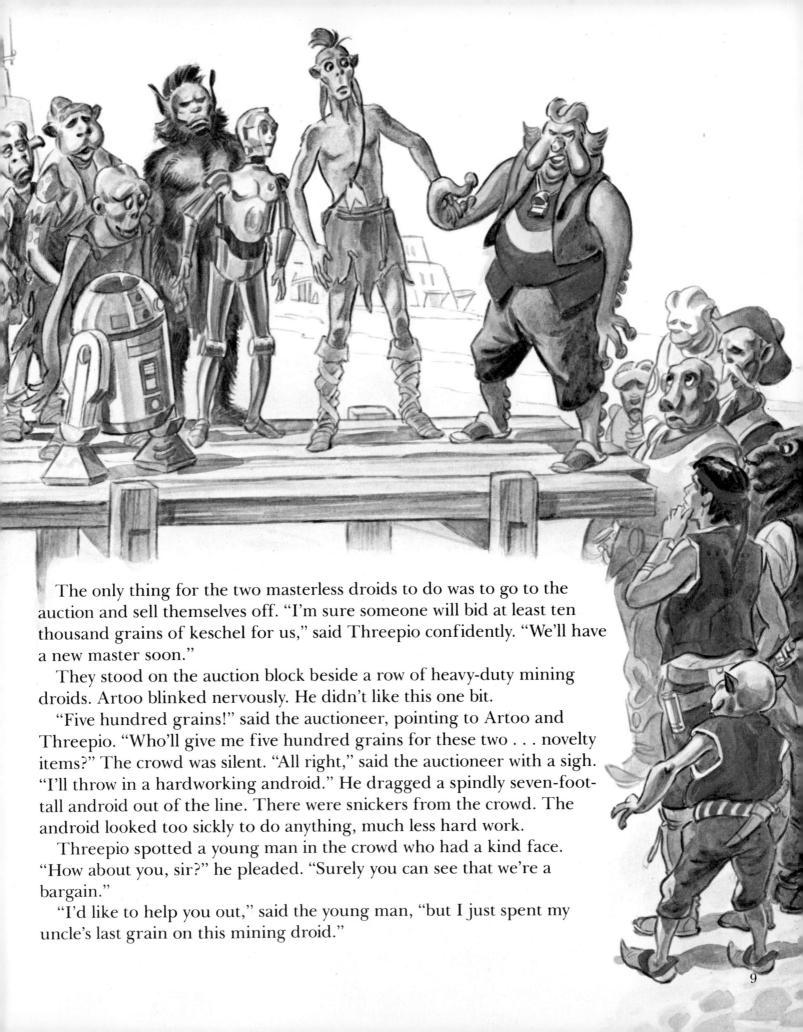

The only thing for the two masterless droids to do was to go to the auction and sell themselves off. "I'm sure someone will bid at least ten thousand grains of keschel for us," said Threepio confidently. "We'll have a new master soon."

They stood on the auction block beside a row of heavy-duty mining droids. Artoo blinked nervously. He didn't like this one bit.

"Five hundred grains!" said the auctioneer, pointing to Artoo and Threepio. "Who'll give me five hundred grains for these two . . . novelty items?" The crowd was silent. "All right," said the auctioneer with a sigh. "I'll throw in a hardworking android." He dragged a spindly seven-foot-tall android out of the line. There were snickers from the crowd. The android looked too sickly to do anything, much less hard work.

Threepio spotted a young man in the crowd who had a kind face. "How about you, sir?" he pleaded. "Surely you can see that we're a bargain."

"I'd like to help you out," said the young man, "but I just spent my uncle's last grain on this mining droid."

Yorpo Mog eyed Artoo and Threepio and a wide grin spread over his ugly face. Here was his chance to get his hands on that miserable little droid who had made him look like a fool. "I take them!" he shouted.

"*Sold!*" said the auctioneer. "To Yorpo Mog, for sixty grains!" Artoo squeaked in terror. As the auctioneer shoved the three of them roughly off the auction block, the sick android keeled over. When he tried to get up, Yorpo kicked him back into the mud with his foot. "Worthless android," he muttered.

"This can't be allowed!" cried the young man. "Man or machine, nothing should be treated like that! Tell Yorpo Mog I'll trade him my three-thousand-keschel mining droid for these three."

Yorpo's eyes widened. He couldn't believe anyone could be so stupid. "Okay," he said.

"Thank the Maker!" cried Threepio. "We have a wonderful new master!"

"Jann Tosh is my name," said the young man, helping the feeble android up. "And my uncle Gundy sure won't think I'm wonderful."

Artoo had been standing close to the android, blinking furiously. Now he began to make excited little whistles and beeps. "My word!" said Threepio. "Artoo says that this android isn't an android at all. He's an organic life form!"

"Well, I'll be darned," said Jann. He piled his new friends into his rusty old roller vehicle, wondering what he was going to tell his uncle about the three-thousand-keschel mining droid.

As they headed out of town Kleb and Yorpo watched them from the shadows. Kleb was furious with his henchman. "*Fool!*" he yelled. "That'zz him! That'zz Julpa! He'zz worth forty thouzzzand grainzz to me, and you traded him for a ztupid mining droid!" He whacked the huge mining droid angrily, and all its circuits exploded at once. Yorpo could only grin sheepishly.

"Don't juzzt zztand there! Go and get him!" shouted Kleb.

Yorpo made a flying leap for the roller, but Jann saw him first. "Threepio! Take the controls!" he shouted. As Threepio frantically tried to control the roller, it shot forward, careened wildly down the street, and knocked Yorpo into the mud.

Kleb was beside himself with rage. "You idiot! You let themmm ezzcape! You muzzzt be punished. I'm going to make you . . . take a *bath*!"

An hour later Jann and his friends finally clanked into Uncle Gundy's mining camp, safe and sound. "Now, remember," Jann warned them, "his bark is worse than his bite."

Gundy came running out of the mine. "Yee-haw!" he yelled. "Let's see that work droid, Jann-boy!"

Jann swallowed hard. "No work droid," he said. "I bought one, but I traded it for these three."

"These three?" echoed Gundy. He was trying to understand how a three-thousand-keschel work droid could have been traded for this ragtag bunch.

"These three," repeated Jann. "I had to. They were in big trouble. But look at the bright side. Now we've got *two* droids instead of one."

"Two prissy droids and a half-starved, half-witted seven-foot varmint? How am I supposed to run a mine with them? Sufferin' satellites, boy, yer always savin' the whole galaxy and leavin' us worse off than we was before!" Gundy flung his hat to the ground in exasperation and stamped on it. When he was all done, Artoo carefully picked it up, dusted it off, and handed it back to Uncle Gundy, whistling timidly.

Gundy tried hard not to smile. "Well, as long as yer here, I guess we'll have to keep you," he said. He turned to Threepio. "Can you cook?" he asked.

"I am well schooled in the preparation of intergalactic cuisine," answered Threepio proudly.

"Well, go to it. Looks like yer friend here could use some grub." The pale stranger was indeed looking wobbly. He did not speak, but his eyes were filled with gratitude.

In the days that followed, Gundy, Jann, and Artoo went off in the mornings to work in the mine. Threepio stayed behind to cook and look after the pale young alien, who soon began to get stronger. He ate Threepio's awful stew hungrily, and the color began to return to his cheeks. He was even able to do a little work around the camp, carrying water for the cooking and washing. Sitting beside Jann for hours, he learned how to repair the ore-cutting machines. Jann was amazed at how quickly he learned, and how patient and gentle he was too. There seemed to be something special about him; even Uncle Gundy felt it. But the stranger's identity remained a mystery. He did not seem to speak any language at all.

"I think I'll call him Kez-Iban," said Threepio one afternoon.

"What's that?" asked Jann.

"It's a Bocce word," explained Threepio. "It means 'he who returns from life's long journey.'"

Jann smiled at his new friend. "Welcome back, Kez," he said. "I don't know where you come from, but I'm glad you're here."

Kez-Iban smiled too, but there was a little bit of sadness in the smile.

Suddenly there was a deep, rumbling roar from the direction of the mine.

"Uncle Gundy!!" yelled Jann. "He's still in the mine! I knew those old timbers were going to give out soon!" They sprinted out to the mine, hardly able to see because of the swirling dust.

"Artoo, shine your light inside," said Jann. The light bounced crazily off the walls. "There he is! I see him!" Gundy was on the floor of the cavern, pinned by a fallen timber.

"Master Jann, I don't recommend that you go in there," said Threepio worriedly. "The ceiling timber is cracked, and the whole roof may come down at any moment."

Without saying a word Kez-Iban drew himself up to his full seven feet, walked into the cavern, and threw his thin shoulder against the ceiling beam. He nodded toward Gundy, his lips pressed tightly together as he strained under the weight.

"Let's go!" shouted Jann, running inside. "Hurry!" With all their strength, he and Threepio lifted the great beam from Gundy's body. Jann glanced at Kez and saw that his lips were white and his legs were shaking.

"Hold on, Kez!" called Jann as he and Threepio carried Gundy out. "I'm coming back for you!"

"No, master, it's not safe!" cried Threepio. But Jann picked up a shoring timber and raced back into the mine.

Inside, Kez-Iban's strength was almost gone. There were low rumbles. The mine seemed to be on the verge of collapsing. Jann shoved the timber into place and tried to wedge it in. "Almost there, Kez," he grunted.

Then Threepio came charging in. "The mine! It's going to—" *Crash!* He tripped over Artoo and went shooting smack into the beam, wedging it firmly into place. They were safe! Kez-Iban, his strength exhausted, dropped to the ground. Jann fell beside him, panting.

Jann reached out and clasped Kez-Iban's hand. "Thank you," he said. "If it hadn't been for you . . ." He couldn't finish.

"Now may I suggest," said Threepio briskly, "that we take Master Gundy into town for medical treatment?"

Back in the town of Tyne's Horky, Kleb Zellock was having a good day. He sat at his usual table at Doodnik's. Across from him was an odd-looking fellow. Very ugly—and very clean. It was Yorpo Mog.

"Well?" demanded Kleb. "Do you havvve it?"

Grinning, Yorpo put a small gray box on the table. He lifted the lid. Inside was a small blue crystal. An eerie, throbbing blue light pulsed from it. Kleb looked at it greedily. "Nergon 14!" He laughed wickedly. "At lazzt it izzz mine!"

Suddenly his face changed and he flung himself to the far end of the booth. "Clozze the box, youu idiot!" he hissed. "That zztuff will contaminate the whole plazze!"

Yorpo slammed the lid down and Kleb collected himself. "Nnoww," he said, "azz I wazz saying . . . we're going to be richhh, Yorpo. Alll we have to doo is finnd zomebody to carry all that nergon out of the minnne for uzz."

He looked out the window just in time to spot Jann and his three friends taking Uncle Gundy to the medical tent.

"Aaah . . ." smiled Kleb. "I think I zzee zome volunteerzz." He pushed the box back to Yorpo. "Youu know what to dooo," he said. "Take thizz with youu . . . and beee careful with it!"

Yorpo eagerly took the box, almost dropping it in his haste.

"I zzaid be careful!" repeated Kleb. "That nergon izz uzzed by the Empire for itz photon torpedoezz! Compared to nergon, keschel izz without value! Now, get goinggg."

Ten minutes later Jann emerged from the medical tent with his uncle. "I knew you'd be fine," Jann was saying. "It'd take more than a cave-in to—" He stopped as Threepio ran up to him in a tizzy. "Master!" Threepio cried. "Yorpo Mog has made off with Kez! There was nothing I could do."

"C'mon!" shouted Jann over his shoulder. "We've got to find him!"

Inside Doodnik's Café, Kleb was still having a good day. Not only did he have the nergon 14, but he also had this Julpa fellow—safely hidden away. A good day indeed. He smiled pleasantly across the table at Sollag, the hooded man who had been so eager to find Kleb's prisoner.

"This is—robbery!" protested Sollag. "We agreed upon a price of forty thousand grains of keschel. You can't demand more now!"

"I cann doo anything I wannt. Ezpecially zzince there are otherzz who would pay a higher prize for your mazzter, I'm zzure."

"Villain!" shouted Sollag. "I'm here to save him! Those others would destroy him!" He leaped across the table at Kleb, but Yorpo easily scooped him up and dangled him in the air. As Sollag's hooded cloak fell aside it revealed a face that looked much like Kez-Iban's. They were of the same alien race.

At that moment Jann came barging into the café. "Put him down, Yorpo!" he yelled. Nobody in the café even looked up. "Kleb, what have you done with Kez?"

Kleb's chuckle turned to a hearty laugh. "I've been expectingg youuuu," he said.

Threepio was watching worriedly. "I have a bad feeling about this situation, Artoo," he whispered. "Do something!"

Artoo turned to a large, hairy, mean-looking miner behind him and made the rudest noise he could, right into the miner's face.

"Why, you little—" roared the enraged miner, swinging for Artoo. But Artoo trundled out of the way at the last second, and the miner belted Yorpo instead. Within seconds the whole place had erupted into an all-out brawl.

Jann grabbed Sollag. "Let's get out of here!" he whispered. The two droids followed, and they all darted out of the bar.

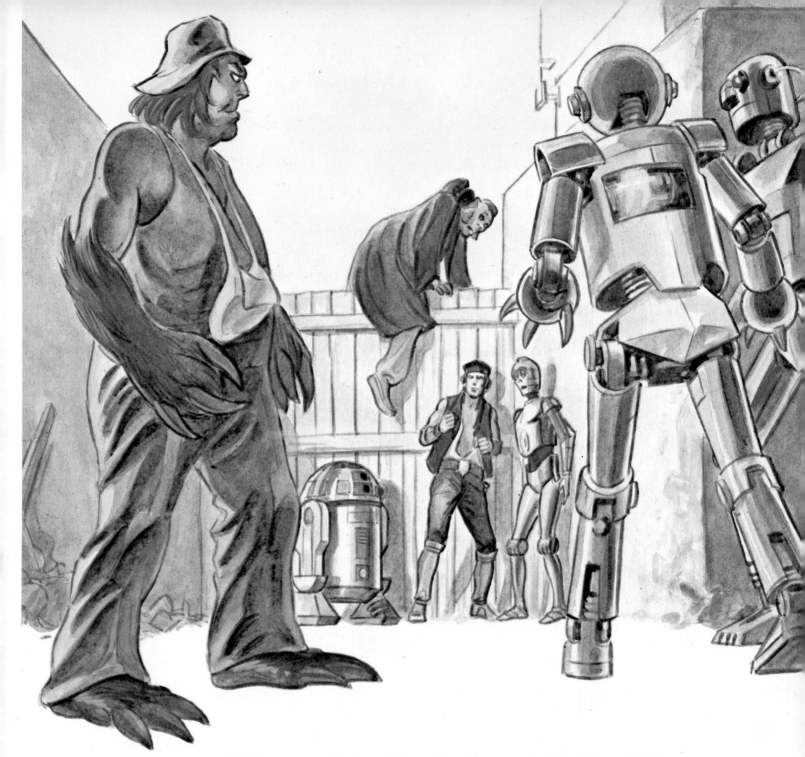

"This way," called Jann, sprinting down the alleyway behind Doodnik's. "I think this leads to"—a tall fence loomed up at the end of the alley— "nowhere," he finished. They all began to run back the other way, only to find their way blocked by Yorpo and two huge mining droids. They were trapped!

In an instant Sollag had leaped onto Artoo and vaulted over the fence. He was gone. "Well," said Jann, shaking his head, "I guess Uncle Gundy is right. That's what comes of helping strangers."

Yorpo laughed evilly as he lumbered toward Jann and the droids.

A few hours later Yorpo removed the blindfolds from Jann and Threepio and peeled off the sticky black patch which had been placed over Artoo's lens. "Where have you taken us?" Jann demanded.

"Oh, dear," said Threepio. "It appears to be some sort of mine. I think we must be in the control room."

"Yourr droid izz correct," said Kleb, from behind them. "It'zz my zzecret little minnne. Welcome."

Jann and the droids looked through the windows of the control room, down into a huge underground cavern. At the bottom, two ore cutters were shooting laser beams to carve out chunks of glowing blue crystals.

"*Nergon?*" said Jann. He couldn't believe his eyes.

Threepio watched the crystals pulsate. "Nergon 14, sir!" he said. "The most dangerous element in the universe!"

"The droid izz right againn," said Kleb. "I zuggezzt you be very careful when you carry it out of the minne for mee."

"*No!*" Jann made a flying leap for Kleb, but he didn't get very far. A high-pitched screech filled the air, of such intensity that Jann fell to the floor, writhing in agony. Kleb closed his mouth.

"Do not dooo that againnn," he warned. "Yorpo, take them away. They begin loading in the morning."

"But he'll be killed!" said Threepio. "Nergon is deadly to humans."

"Yezz, I know," Kleb replied cheerfully as he left.

Hours later Jann awoke on the floor of the cavern. There was a tremendous bump on his head, and he felt awful. He looked around through a fog. A tall, hazy figure was standing over him.

"Kez!" Jann was overjoyed to see his friend. "Are you all right?"

Kez-Iban put a finger to his lips and pointed to a mining droid standing guard outside the chamber. Then he pointed down. Jann saw that his leg was shackled to Kez's by a length of electrical cable, and Kez's leg was attached to Threepio's in the same way. But it was only Threepio's *leg*— the rest of him was in the corner, working with Artoo.

"We're almost done, sir," whispered Threepio. "Artoo is shutting down the power to the electrical leg shackles. Then we can safely cut them."

A blaster shot whined off the wall beside them. It was the gigantic mining droid! It moved toward them, taking more careful aim. There was no way they could fight a droid that powerful.

Suddenly a dark figure dropped onto the droid's back and began to pound at it. For a split second the droid's attention was diverted. This was Jann's chance. He grabbed Threepio's abandoned leg and swung it at the droid's blaster. The blaster went off, sending a wild shot up to the ceiling. A huge chunk of rock came loose and hurtled with a crash onto the

mining droid. The droid stiffened and went down, its circuits fizzing and popping.

"Whew!" breathed the dark figure, crawling out from under the droid. It was Sollag.

"I had to let them capture you," he panted, "so I could follow . . . I have to find . . ."

Suddenly his eyes landed on Kez. A look of shocked surprise spread across his face. The same look was on Kez's face.

"*Mon Julpa!*" cried Sollag. He fell to his knees before Kez, his forehead on the ground.

A strange look of recollection now passed over Kez's features. "Mon Julpa," he repeated thoughtfully.

Sollag produced a long, burnished green scepter. At its head was a beautiful glowing gem. As the light from the gem flickered over Kez's face, his expression changed. He was remembering. He no longer looked vague and confused; he looked like a prince.

"Ma Sollag. Neinspenfaah na Mon Julpa!" said Sollag, in awe.

Kez drew himself up to his full height. "Ne-Yot!" he said. "Ma sa Julpa aug Tammuz!"

Threepio translated in hushed tones. " 'I hold the royal scepter of Tammuz-An.' "

"Royal?" whispered Jann. "Does that mean he's a— a—"

"A prince," said Threepio.

Artoo interrupted with urgent beeping and clicking. He had just finished cutting their electrical cables with his little buzz saw, but he had detected a new problem.

"Artoo says that there are dangerous levels of explosive gas in the cavern," explained Threepio, hurriedly reattaching his leg. "If it's sparked by those laser cutters, it could well activate the nergon!"

Indeed, the nergon looked different. The blue crystals were beginning to give off a pulsing, throbbing light.

"We've got to get out of here!" cried Jann. "Quick—the elevators to the control tower!" They all began to run for the elevator.

"Jann! Look out!" warned Sollag. Jann turned to see a heavily armed mining droid almost upon him. Before he could react, the droid had thrown out one of its huge armlike parts and knocked him sprawling to the ground. It held him there, pinned and helpless.

Artoo beeped another warning. "The gas levels are still rising," said Threepio. "And the cutters are still cutting!"

Out of the corner of his eye Jann saw Kez-Iban lift his scepter and point it at the head of the droid. A strange, sparkly ray shot out. Instantly the droid began to smoke and spark, and then it went limp. Jann scrambled from under the inert arm. "Thanks—again!" he said to Kez. "Now, let's get out of here!"

They ran to the elevator and piled in.

In a moment the doors were opening onto the control tower. Kleb was waiting calmly for them, Yorpo beside him.

"Kleb, you've got to shut those cutters off!" said Jann. "The nergon is about to blow!"

"I'll doo no zzuch thing," hissed Kleb. "Annd youu are getting in my wayy." He opened his mouth, and the terrible screech issued forth. Jann, Kez, and Sollag fell to the ground.

"Kleb! Look!" said Yorpo in horror. "The nergon!" The blue crystals in the cavern below were pulsing faster and faster. "We have to get out of here!"

"What do you meannn, *we*?" asked Kleb evilly. "Perhapzz it izz time for me to go, but youuu will zztay here with the otherzz. There'zz only enough keschel for me, youu zzeee." As he spoke, there was a great booming from the cavern below. The nergon was now glowing a deep, steady red!

"I'lll be goingg now," said Kleb. He turned and ran out of the control room.

"After him!" said Jann.

They raced after Kleb down a dark, winding tunnel. Yorpo led the way, showing them where to turn whenever the tunnel forked. They ran through tunnel after tunnel, until they felt their lungs would burst. At last they reached their destination—a high, windswept gyrocopter pad. Kleb was loading a pile of large bundles into the copter as they arrived.

"You—stop!" bellowed Yorpo, zapping Kleb with his stunner. Kleb slumped, unconscious, and Yorpo rushed past him and began to climb into the copter. But Artoo was right behind him.

"Yeeow!" yelled Yorpo. Artoo had given him a little electrical shock, just enough to slow him down so that Jann and the others could pile into the gyrocopter too.

"Hurry, Master Kez," urged Threepio as Jann dragged Kleb aboard. "The nergon is about to blow sky-high!"

Jann tried lifting the copter off the pad, but something was stopping it. "We're too heavy," he said. "Throw those bundles out!" Threepio threw them overboard, and the copter rose into the sky just as a huge explosion rocked the mines.

"Thank the Maker," said Threepio with a sigh. "We're safe!"

"Yes," said Jann. "Thanks to you and Artoo and Kez—I mean Mon Julpa—and Sollag. True friends, all of you."

Artoo bleeped and flashed. "He says," translated Threepio, "that we should expect Kleb to be very angry when he wakes up. Those bundles you jettisoned back there—that was all his keschel. His entire fortune."

The next day, back at Uncle Gundy's mine, it was time to say good-bye. Gundy was trying hard to understand.

"You say Kez here's an honest-to-pete king?" he said, scratching his grizzled head.

"A prince," corrected Sollag. "When our world's evil traitors took his throne, they erased his mind and left him to die."

"Thanks to you and your droids," said Mon Julpa, "my memory is restored. Now I must return to my people and my throne."

"And if it weren't for that cave-in, and you savin' me, I never would have found that vein of keschel in the mine. We're rich now! I'm mighty grateful to you, Kez. I mean—Prince Kez," said Gundy.

"You see, Artoo," said Threepio happily, "I knew we'd find a wealthy master. Our troubles are over."

"That doesn't mean ya don't have to work, ya varmints. Ya still have to replace that minin' droid! Now, git to it, before I—"

This time Artoo didn't wait for Gundy to throw down his hat and stamp on it. The little droid reached up, removed Gundy's hat, put it carefully on the ground, and stamped on it himself. And this time, everybody laughed!